Trapped in Battle Royale
Book Three

BETRAYAL AT SALTY SPRINGS

AN UNOFFICIAL NOVEL FOR FORTNITE FANS

Devin Hunter

Sky Pony Press
New York

Copyright © 2018 by Hollan Publishing, Inc.

Fortnite® is a registered trademark of Epic Games, Inc.

The Fortnite game is copyright © Epic Games, Inc.

All rights reserved. No part of this book may be reproduced in any manner
without the express written consent of the publisher, except in the case of
brief excerpts in critical reviews or articles. All inquiries should be addressed
to Sky Pony Press, 307 West 36th Street, 11th Floor, New York, NY 10018.

Sky Pony Press books may be purchased in bulk at special discounts for sales
promotion, corporate gifts, fund-raising, or educational purposes. Special
editions can also be created to specifications. For details, contact the Special
Sales Department, Sky Pony Press, 307 West 36th Street, 11th Floor,
New York, NY 10018 or info@skyhorsepublishing.com.

Sky Pony® is a registered trademark of Skyhorse Publishing, Inc.®,
a Delaware corporation.

Visit our website at www.skyponypress.com.

10 9 8 7 6 5 4 3 2

Library of Congress Cataloging-in-Publication Data is available on file.

Series design by Brian Peterson
Cover artwork by Amanda Brack

Paperback ISBN: 978-1-5107-4344-1
E-book ISBN: 978-1-5107-4345-8

Printed in Canada

CHAPTER 1

After a week of practices with Hans's squad, Grey knew he'd gotten better at almost every aspect of Fortnite Battle Royale. As he dueled Hans in building practice, the walls and counter-ramps went up almost without Grey thinking. It was already becoming second nature, though Hans always gave him a tough battle.

Even now, Grey struggled to get the high ground on Hans. They remained even, both having gotten a few shots on each other.

Grey could have gained the high ground quicker, but he was challenging himself to use fewer materials than usual. He had to learn how to be more efficient in times when he was starved

1

for mats, which would likely be more often now because there was a patch tomorrow.

And that patch was nerfing material drops in llamas, among other things.

Now instead of getting five hundred wood, brick, and metal from a llama, there would only be two hundred of each. None of the one hundred players stuck in this virtual reality version of Fortnite Battle Royale were happy about it. But the Admin only announced changes, and there was no way to argue with what had been decided.

They would all have to adapt.

On top of the materials nerf, some of the favorite weapons were getting altered as well. Many people trapped here had long preferred the AR weapons, but this patch would bring a big damage and speed reduction to them. People were already trying to rely more on their shotguns. The patch was also buffing the submachine gun category, so people were practicing with those instead.

The Admin also announced there would be "trouble" on the map. No one was sure exactly what that meant, but the players who had been stuck in the game for several seasons said it was probably a hint for map changes.

Grey was growing impatient with Hans, so he dropped a bounce pad and built a floor under him to get higher. It put him in an exposed position, but he aimed right for Hans. Grey's shotgun connected, and he dropped another bounce pad on his newly made floor to jump even higher.

The best part about bounce pads, according to Grey, was that you didn't take fall damage when you used them. Instead of building higher, he wanted to use the structure they'd already built below instead of burning through more materials.

Grey let off several shots, but only a couple of them hit Hans as Grey was dropping down over six stories. He expected Hans to follow him, so he switched from placing bounce pads to placing traps and put one on a wall. Hans was probably too smart to fall for it, but Grey still wanted to try. It could fool a less skilled player.

Hans jumped away, but Grey quickly threw a bounce pad on the opposing wall so that Hans bounced right back into the trap.

"You!" Hans let out a surprised laugh. "Good move! I'm calling that a win for you."

"It was a good fight," Grey said. It always felt good to win in practice, but he didn't want to act too confident. "It could have easily gone the other way."

"That extra bounce was clever," Hans said. "Did you plan that?"

Grey shrugged. "It wasn't exactly in the plan."

"You are good at thinking on your feet." Hans looked up at the giant build they had made together. "If I didn't already know your answer, I'd ask you to fill my last squad spot."

Grey felt his face grow warm. It was a huge compliment, and he still hadn't gotten used to people asking him to join up with them. But Hans was right—Grey had no interest in leaving his squad behind. He, Kiri, Ben, and Tristan had made so much progress together he couldn't imagine flying into battles with anyone else.

Besides, they were closing in on the top twenty in rank.

As it stood today, they were in the top twenty-five, and Grey had high hopes of breaking into the twenties this week. They already had gotten several more Victory Royales, and that had earned them practices with not just Hans's squad but also Zach's squad.

People complimented Grey on his tactical skills, Ben on his close-range fighting, Tristan on his in-depth game knowledge, and Kiri on her exceptional aim. In fact, she'd grown so notorious for her sniper shots that some even whispered she'd be better than Tae Min in no time.

Tae Min did not agree, making sure to personally take Kiri out at every opportunity.

"Grey, I won!" Kiri yelled as she came running from her own build battle with Mayumi. "Can you even believe it? I never win!"

"Nice!" He held up his hand for a high five.

"She got lucky," Mayumi said with a sour look. "I had nine shots on her."

"But I still got ten first!" Kiri bounced around. Building had never been her strong suit, but she had gotten a lot better through practice.

Not looking nearly as excited, Tristan arrived from his build battle with Farrah. He'd obviously lost, because he ignored the topic in general and said, "Where's Ben?"

"Not sure. Just finished up." Grey scanned the busy practice area. They had already finished games for the day, so there were a lot of people outside the practice warehouse building. Grey never thought he'd belong here—they used to go out much farther to practice—but most people now greeted their squad with a smile and wave.

After a few seconds, Grey spotted Ben chatting with Zach. They weren't doing anything in particular, so Grey called out, "Ben! Your turn!"

Ben nodded at Grey, running over with a big smile on his face. "Who do I get to duel?"

"Mayumi and I lost," Hans said. "So take your pick."

"You *lost*?" Ben looked at Grey. "Nice job, Grey."

"He played smart," Hans said.

"Or you picked up some bad luck," Ben said. "I better duel you to make sure."

Hans smiled. "All right, then."

"Rematch?" Mayumi asked Kiri.

"Yeah, mate!" Kiri said with a smile. Mayumi was actually pretty nice, a high school girl from Japan who had just moved to Australia before she got sucked into the game. She'd been stuck there for three seasons.

Tristan and Farrah, a college student from Turkey, also set up a rematch, so Grey was the odd one out for this round.

They didn't have much more time left before everyone had to be in their cabins, so Grey figured that would be his last practice run for the day. It would have been nice if they had even numbers in both their squads, but Hans's squad still often beat them as it was. Grey couldn't imagine how it would be if Hans had a full four.

Grey headed back to his cabin, the mental fatigue of the day weighing on him. While he'd gotten more used to leading his squad, it was still hard to accept at times. He wished he could take a break from it. From the whole game, really. It had been a month of his life now, and it was exhausting.

As he approached his cabin, Grey paused before he went inside because he heard voices. One unmistakable voice in particular:

Hazel's.

CHAPTER 2

For a second Grey thought he might have gone to the wrong cabin, but as he moved closer to the door, he understood why Hazel was there.

"C'mon, Tae Min!" Hazel's voice wasn't as angry as Grey had thought he heard, but there was still an edge to it. "I know you think you're above all this, but can't you help me out? I've heard the story from everyone, how to tank your score to stay. I *need* to get back this season."

"Everyone says that," Tae Min says. "You're no different."

"My dad is dying!" Hazel said. "Have you no heart?"

Grey's eyes widened. Hazel hadn't said

anything about her life that wasn't bragging about how good she was at Fortnite. At least not that Grey had heard, though they had been rivals since they both appeared in this virtual reality a month ago.

But her dad was dying . . . Grey suddenly felt bad for Hazel for the first time since he'd been here. He hadn't even felt bad for her when she'd gotten kicked out of her squad a week ago. It hadn't impacted her rank much. She was still in the thirties.

"You're lying," Tae Min replied. "You're the one with no heart. And your attempt at manipulating my emotions is another low."

"Ugh, fine! I'm lying." There was a long pause, and Grey wondered how Tae Min had known Hazel was lying. Grey had been fooled so easily. He had to remember there was no real way to know what any of these people did in real life. "But that's how you pick, right? Whoever has the biggest sob story wins your free pass. That's what everyone says."

"I don't know what you're talking about," Tae Min said.

"Now who's lying?" Hazel let out a frustrated grunt. "You're so selfish!"

Grey heard stomping footsteps, and he rushed to hide behind a nearby bush. The last thing he wanted was for Hazel to see him eavesdropping. For the last week, it had been nice to have her largely out of his mind. With no squad and a lower rank than Grey, she had turned her trolling ways to other, lower-ranked players.

He watched as she trudged out of his cabin. Her face wore the usual angry expression as she disappeared into her own lodgings. He waited a few more seconds before he went to his own cabin, just to make sure Tae Min didn't suspect Grey was eavesdropping either. Though maybe Tae Min still would . . . After all, he could some-how see through Hazel's lying.

Grey only glanced at Tae Min as he made his way to his bed. They hadn't spoken since that one time when Tae Min had told Grey to build smarter and not just faster. It was that one small bit of advice, Grey felt, that had propelled him to the next level in the game. He'd wanted to thank Tae Min for it, but he didn't know how to start a conversation with the guy. Most people who tried to talk to Tae Min left in a frustrated way like Hazel did. The only time Grey had ever seen it go well was when Tae Min was the first to talk.

"You're doing better," Tae Min said out of nowhere.

"Trying to." Grey took a deep breath, since he might not get another chance. "Thanks. You know, for the advice."

Tae Min nodded once, his shoulder-length black hair hiding part of his face. "The patch will be annoying. Lots of people will be whining about it."

"They already are," Grey said. Tae Min's words didn't sound like advice, but Grey still was curious. It felt like Tae Min was trying to make conversation.

"Ranks will slip. People will fight. Squads will split up," Tae Min said. "It happens every time there is a patch."

"I see . . ." A twinge of nerves hit Grey. While he wasn't concerned with his own squad fighting, he hadn't thought about how hard patches might be. This was his first one. He'd finally gotten close to the top twenty—would that change now? Could a materials nerf and AR damage reduction really change things so much? "I don't like when people fight like that. It's enough to fight in the battles every day."

"No squad can stay together forever," Tae

Min said. "Either you split up here. Or you split up when you go home."

Grey didn't know how to respond to this. It felt like Tae Min was trying to warn him, which Grey appreciated, but there was no way his squad would split. They'd soared in the ranks. Everyone was working together. There wasn't anything to fight about.

But Tae Min did have a point—if Grey's squad made it out, they'd all be separated. In some cases by giant oceans.

He couldn't play with them forever.

Maybe that was what Tae Min was trying to say. Grey couldn't get too attached if he wanted to keep his eye on the prize, which was getting home. He still wanted that, even if his homesickness had eased up a lot.

If Grey was being honest with himself, he *had* gotten attached to his squad mates here in the game. They'd become his friends and the closest he had to a family while stuck here. He didn't want to lose them once any of them escaped the game. He'd have to find a way to bring that up to them and see if they could stay in contact even after they got out.

"You are too kind," Tae Min said. "I'm sorry

people will take advantage of that until you learn who to trust."

This comment only confused Grey more. He had no idea what Tae Min was really trying to tell him. Maybe he wasn't speaking about Grey at all, but referring to his conversation with Hazel to see if Grey had overheard. Or maybe, like usual, Tae Min saw something Grey didn't.

If that was the case, Grey worried he wouldn't catch Tae Min's true meaning until it was too late.

CHAPTER 3

The mood in the battle warehouse on patch day was eerily quiet. Grey expected it to be more excited, but things felt different right from the moment his squad gathered together. He felt like he had to offer some words of encouragement, even if he didn't think this patch would be a big deal. "We can do this, guys. We just need to find the right weapons and farm enough mats, just like normal."

Kiri nodded. "Right."

Ben didn't look so sure. "AR was my best weapon."

"You'll be great with anything you pick up," Grey said. "You've gotten a lot better with all our practice against Hans's squad."

"Let's hope so . . ." Ben glanced at Tristan, who didn't seem nervous about the patch.

"We will do great," Tristan said. "Grey and Kiri are best on shotguns and snipers, so they won't be fazed at all as long as they get materials."

"It's not like we get llamas all the time," Kiri said. "It'll work out!"

Ben nodded. "Yeah . . ."

Before they could say anything else, the Admin appeared and they all teleported to the ranking line. Even though the Admin always appeared friendly and smiling, with her nice suit and pinned-up blonde hair, Grey had only grown to dislike her more. He still wasn't sure if she was a computer program or a real person, but he had a feeling there was *someone* behind that avatar.

"Welcome to Day Thirty of Battles, players!" the Admin said. "Today is patch day. The game has been updated during your rest, and all aforementioned changes have been implemented on the island. If you notice any bugs, please notify me immediately after any battle by using the Report Bug icon available in your vision selection. We will work quickly to correct any issues, if they are valid and not in line with the patch's intended working order. Good luck in today's battles!"

The Admin disappeared, and the familiar deep voice announced, "Thirty seconds until the next battle!"

"Salty Springs," Grey said as he leaned in to give his squad one last encouraging smile. "We got this, okay?"

Ben looked like he didn't believe Grey at all. "Good luck, G—"

Grey's vision went black, something he'd gotten used to as a signal he was teleporting wherever the game wanted him at the time. It never took long, but today it felt a smidge lengthier than usual. Maybe because of the patch.

When Grey appeared in the Battle Bus, nothing felt different. Maybe it was a new patch, but so far it was still the game he'd been stuck in for the last month. All the boxes for inventory and materials looked the same in his vision, but then he noticed something strange on the left side.

Only Kiri's name appeared in his squad.

Maybe it was a bug. Like the Admin had said.

"Ben? Tristan?" Grey called out. "You there? Your names aren't showing in my squad list."

"Not in mine, either," Kiri said. "Weird."

"Ben? Tristan?" Grey repeated as his panic began to rise.

"C'mon, mates," Kiri said. "Stop joking around. If you're there, say it. We really can't see you."

There was no answer.

"Do you think they can't see us, either?" Kiri asked.

"I don't know . . ." Grey's heart rate skyrocketed as players began to jump from the bus. As much as he wanted to believe this was some kind of bug, suddenly everything Tae Min had said last night began to make sense.

No squad stays together forever.

You're too kind.

People will take advantage of that.

This could not be happening. When Tristan had left his former squad in the first week, he had told Ben he was doing it. Tristan didn't just disappear. If Ben and Tristan had plans to leave, wouldn't they have told Grey? And why would they leave when their ranks had gotten so high already?

"Grey, we gotta jump," Kiri said. "Bus is almost done flying."

"Right." Grey stood from his seat and moved to the back to jump out. No one else was still on the bus. They were over Retail Row, so they could still easily fly to Salty Springs from here. "Maybe they're just as confused as we are?"

"I reckon," Kiri said. "Nothing we can do about it now."

He jumped out and Kiri followed right behind. There were several people in the air below them, and he paid attention to where they landed so he'd have a good idea of where enemy players might come from. Several dropped in Retail Row, but there were many that went for Salty Springs and Dusty Divot.

He and Kiri broke open a roof as the sound of a treasure chest filled his ears. They opened the chest and moved quickly through the house. They ended up with a shotgun and two ARs . . . which wasn't a good haul with the new patch. Grey had gathered extra materials and they both had a shield, but it felt weird to only be with Kiri. He had kept an eye out on the map, hoping to see Ben's and Tristan's names pop up in his vision even if they weren't shown on his squad list. That would at least mean they were still paired up.

There were no names.

It was further proof that Ben and Tristan might not be in their squad at all, but Grey still held out the smallest hope that this was all a bug. A mistake. Something that meant Ben and Tristan hadn't just left him with no explanation.

"Incoming from the south, sounds like," Kiri said as they looted another house.

The gunfire grew louder, and Grey peeked out a window. Kiri was right.

"Four." Usually Grey wasn't afraid of a full squad, but that was when he had his own to rely on. He wasn't sure how to fight with just two of them. Especially when they still weren't particularly well-geared.

"What do we do?" Kiri asked, a clear strain of fear in her voice.

"Shoot." Grey held up the AR to shoot some rounds from the window. They hit, but the lack of damage was clear. Normally, he would have had that player down—not this time. He took return damage, instinctively threw up a wall, and ran deeper into the house.

Kiri followed, but Grey already knew it'd be over when he heard the distinct click of the C4. It detonated, and the building crumbled as Grey's vision went black and white. As he stared at the notification on his screen, he wished he didn't know how to read.

Ben eliminated you.

Ben eliminated Kiri.

"What the . . . ?" Kiri yelled. "They left us? Why would they leave us and not say anything? How could they even do that without us knowing?"

Grey wanted to ask them all the same questions, but then he thought about how Ben had been acting before the battles. "It wasn't nerves over the patch . . . They planned this. They must have dropped just before the battle started."

"Who would they even go with? No top squad has two spots open!" Kiri said.

That was true, but a thought came to mind. "Doesn't mean people didn't plan to change things up last night. Ben was talking to Zach, right?"

"Right . . ." Kiri sounded like she was on the verge of crying, so Grey knew she was probably as much in the dark about this as he was. "But why would they not tell us? How could they leave like this? It's so mean."

"To tank our rank this battle at least," Grey replied. It was ruthless, but as he looked at his rank in the eighties for this game he was certain that was part of the plan. Throw him and Kiri off, make sure they dropped out of the top twenty-five. He was tempted to spectate Ben and see if he could figure out who else was in the squad, but part of him just couldn't do it.

The betrayal already hurt too much.

Watching would make him feel even more sick.

So Grey stayed on the spectating screen, not picking any one to watch. He'd wait until the battle was over, and then . . . He didn't know what he'd do when he'd have to face his "friends."

Kiri gasped. "They're with Zach and Hui Yin! But where did Rafael go?"

Grey didn't reply. He'd take the information Kiri supplied, but he didn't have the energy to ask questions or investigate himself. All he could think was that Ben and Tristan didn't have faith in him even after how hard they'd all worked. Zach's squad was in the top fifteen. That was much closer to the top five they needed to get home, which was more important to Ben and Tristan than sticking it out with Grey.

"Ugh, Rafael is with Hans's squad now," Kiri said. "They must have all moved around to form even squads. When did they plan this?"

Grey began to wonder if it had been in the plans all along, or if it had been more recent. Ben and Tristan had waited until Grey helped them get better, and once they were, they moved on. He couldn't stop thinking about what Tae Min had said last night about people taking advantage of Grey. Tae Min had known. Grey wasn't sure how he'd known, because Tae Min didn't play those sorts of games with people. But he somehow saw it. Maybe he'd seen Ben and Tristan do it in past seasons, even.

"Grey?" Kiri's voice broke through his thoughts. "Are you okay?"

"No" was all he could say back. He wanted to shrug it off. He wanted to easily move on like Ben and Tristan obviously could.

But Grey was not okay. He didn't know how to be even the littlest bit okay.

CHAPTER 4

Ben and Tristan finished in the top ten, their squad right behind Tae Min. Grey was glad Tae Min had taken them out so they didn't win. Grey's bitterness had only festered as the game went on, and by the time everyone was back in the battle warehouse, all he could do was run out before anyone spoke.

Because he didn't want to hear the gossip. He didn't want to hear whatever Ben's and Tristan's excuses would be.

What did any of that matter?

They had made their choice. Had left the squad. Had done it in the meanest way possible without even the decency to warn Grey and Kiri.

Grey ran deep into the forest by the cabins. It

didn't sound like anyone had followed him, and he was grateful Kiri understood he needed to be alone.

Grey went so far that he ran into an invisible barrier that stopped him in his tracks. He fell to the ground but got back up and pushed at the barrier. Soon he was hitting it, screaming at it to let him out. He didn't want to be there from the beginning, and right now he would rather be anywhere else. Maybe there was another game the Admin had. He would take a different cage if that's what it took to get away from these people.

All the liars. Betrayers. Trolls.

No wonder Tae Min played alone.

"Get me out of here!" he yelled at the barrier. "Aren't there any other places you can trap me?"

No one answered. The Admin didn't show up with an offer that would save him from the next battle.

He kicked the barrier one last time before he sat down. He wasn't physically tired—he hadn't felt that in a month—but his mind was exhausted. If only there were a pause button in this game. The brief hour before the next battle didn't feel like nearly enough to gather his composure and pretend he wasn't hurt.

Grey heard footsteps, and he groaned. "Go away, Kiri."

But it wasn't Kiri. Instead, Tae Min appeared from behind some trees. Without saying anything, he sat next to Grey and leaned against the barrier. Grey didn't know what to make of it, but as he looked at Tae Min's solemn profile, it felt like there was sympathy in his expression.

"How did you know?" Grey finally asked. "Did you hear them talking about it?"

Tae Min shook his head. "My real life was filled with people who were only nice to me because they wanted something from me. It's the same here. Everyone wants to use me."

"But I'm not good like you," Grey replied. "Ben and Tristan helped me at first."

"They needed more people in their squad. It benefitted them, and it benefitted them more the faster you improved," Tae Min said. "They will take what you taught them to their new squad and use it to make sure you can't beat them."

It was a heartless way to look at it, but at the moment it felt like everything Tae Min said was true. But Grey still didn't understand. "Why not just fight *with* me, though? We were ranking up. We had a chance."

"You're new." Tae Min leaned forward with a sigh. "No one thinks the newest players deserve to go home. They will admit you are good, but they were here first, and that means they deserve those spots more."

Grey let out a long sigh. He could see that. It wasn't even that he disagreed, but it still made him mad. "It's not fair."

"Of course not. But that's the game."

"Unless you're you," Grey said.

It was the first time Grey saw a wisp of a smile on Tae Min's face. He reached out and ruffled Grey's hair. "You remind me of my little brother."

Grey felt his eyebrows rise. He was more than surprised to hear Tae Min say anything about his real life, since no one knew much about him. Some said he had no family. Some said he stayed here because his real life was crap. But from the small pieces Grey had seen, he knew it had to be more complicated than that.

"You either keep fighting, or you give up," Tae Min said as he stood up. "You don't have any other options."

Tae Min walked away before Grey could give an answer.

Grey knew he was right, but he was just so tired of fighting. It had already been hard enough. Now . . .

"There you are!" Kiri said as she appeared through the trees. "If it weren't for Tae Min, I don't think I'd have found you!"

He still didn't want to face Kiri. If Ben and Tristan could leave, then she could, too. She'd had more offers than all of them combined. Anger welled up as he said, "You can go find a new squad, too. You don't have to stay because you feel bad for me or whatever."

Kiri stopped walking and glared at him. "I'm not leaving. I like playing with you, okay? And you're really good, Grey. You're stuck with me."

"That means you'll be here for another full season at this rate," Grey answered. He had hoped to make top five just yesterday, but today it felt impossible. "Another squad could get you home."

Kiri's shoulders slumped. "I don't think so, mate. We might be good . . . but I'm not stupid. Haven't you noticed who are in those newly made squads?"

Grey shook his head. "I'm pretending they don't exist, remember?"

"Right." Kiri came closer and sat down. "Well, they've all been around since the first and second seasons. Season three at the latest. Hazel got kicked from her squad, too. I don't think it's a coincidence that they're cutting out the newest players. Bet Lorenzo's squad drops him at some point if they have a chance to get a higher rank. Robert still doesn't have one."

"Tae Min said that, too," Grey said.

Kiri looked at him curiously. "He talked to you?"

"He does sometimes," Grey admitted. "I try not to bother him, though."

She nudged him. "You should've asked if he'd be in our squad."

Grey shook his head, thinking of how Tae Min said everyone only wants stuff from him. "He already knows everyone would take him if he wanted—no point in asking. He'd offer if he wanted a squad."

"I guess that's true," Kiri said. "Well, a lot of other people were asking if we'd take them for our squad. You know, if you want."

Grey was honestly surprised to hear it. He couldn't picture anyone wanting to be in his squad when he'd started out so badly. It made him feel a little better, but he also didn't trust any of those people. They wanted to use him like Ben and Tristan, and he was tired of being used. "Is it okay if we think about it for a day at least?"

"Of course," Kiri said. "I'm not in the mood

to take on new people who see us as a stepping ladder, either."

Grey surprised himself by smiling. So Kiri understood at least. Maybe he could trust her in the end, even though he felt like he wasn't good at reading people at all. "Is it okay if we stay here for the day? I can't deal with everyone and also face the battles. Honestly, I don't want to do either."

"Sure, mate," Kiri said. "It's unfair they don't give us days off."

"If only." Grey leaned his head back on the barrier, feeling more trapped than he ever had before. But the next battle would soon be announced, and he would have to fight when all he wanted to do was dive to the ground and face-plant so he didn't have to play.

But he couldn't do that to Kiri. Not when she was sticking with him. There was also a tiny part of him that wanted to prove he didn't need Ben and Tristan to do well. But another part worried they were the only reason Grey had gotten so high in the ranks.

The only way to find out was to keep trying and not give up.

CHAPTER 5

The second and third battles went only slightly better than their battle of betrayal at Salty Springs. While Kiri still got several good kills, they lacked the building power and knowledge that Ben and Tristan had brought to the squad. That combined with the nerfed llamas and ARs, and Grey hadn't managed ranking higher than fifty.

It was now their fourth battle. Grey and Kiri had survived into the forties, but as they ran for the safe zone in Risky Reels, he already saw several large structures and heard the frenzied fighting.

"That's at least two and a half squads," Kiri said.

"We need to lie low for a bit," Grey said as they made it inside the safe zone. They had taken some damage from the storm, so he built a box to protect them and dropped a spare campfire to heal them.

"Stealthy style, ay?" Kiri said as she replenished her shield, which she'd lost when they faced the last duo they eliminated.

"I guess," he replied. "We gotta be smart about the fights we take for now."

"It's a good thing you forced me to learn to build at all . . . Imagine if you hadn't." Kiri's voice had turned somber as she spoke. "Sorry I'm still a bit rubbish."

"You keep getting better," Grey said. *And at least you won't learn and leave like some people.* Grey couldn't help remembering how Tristan and Ben fought about Ben's tendency to "take in strays" who left them for better squads. Now they had done just what they'd complained about.

Grey tried to shake it off. He had to find a way to a safer position. They needed to figure out how to duo well. So far, he couldn't deny they were just plain weaker without their full group.

"We gotta get to higher ground," Kiri said.

"I agree." Grey scanned the area. Risky Reels

wasn't much for high ground unless you built it. But there were some hills and mountains on the Wailing Woods side. Maybe if they could build up there. "Let's try to get to that cliff by Wailing."

"Got it."

Grey edited his box and began the run—and just in time, too, since someone had spotted the box and opened fire on it. Another moment later, the fire was directed at them, and they used walls to protect them as they ran.

Eventually, the shooters gave up, but Grey now knew that didn't mean people weren't keeping an eye on their location. It only meant there was a more imminent threat they had to take care of first.

The fire echoed throughout the area, but then there was silence after a list of elimination notifications.

That was when Kiri yelled, "Launch pad! They're on to us!"

Grey looked over his shoulder, and, sure enough, four players flew in the air. They were incoming fast, so he pulled out the SMG he'd gotten and took aim. If this was where the battle would end, maybe he could get a couple more down.

One took enough damage to fall from their glider and be eliminated, but the others landed and used walls to shield themselves. Grey put down some ramps and ran up to gain the higher ground. He had a few grenades, and he threw them into the squad. Kiri followed behind, and together they were able to take out the whole squad. It felt good, knowing they could still take out a squad even if they were only two people. He would have never been able to do that a month ago.

But the triumph didn't last long. Another squad moved into the fight and launched rockets at them, and while Grey and Kiri tried to heal, they were found by yet another duo.

Elimination was inevitable.

Grey finished at rank thirty-nine and Kiri at thirty-eight. It was the best of the day, but not nearly as good as Grey was now used to.

Their fifth and final game of the day went just about the same. When Grey appeared in the battle warehouse for the end-of-day business, he dreaded what those games would do to his and Kiri's rankings.

Sure enough, Grey didn't stand by his former squad mates anymore. He and Kiri were several people down. Ben and Tristan had moved up, since their new squad had finished top ten in at least three of the games.

A painful concoction of anger and jealousy whirled around in Grey. Seeing those ranks only rubbed in the betrayal that much more. Grey had cared about trying to help Ben and Tristan get home—but they obviously didn't care about him getting home in return. Grey didn't want to stay in line. He didn't want to practice. He didn't want to go back to his cabin where he'd still have to face Ben and Tristan.

He wanted to run away again, but when he tried, he discovered his legs were stuck there.

The Admin appeared. "I hope you all enjoyed playing on the new patch. Some of you observed there was a rocket now stationed at the mountain lab, so we are informing the rest of you in case you would like to observe it. This rocket will be launched during the season, marking incoming changes to the game for the next season."

Several people talked excitedly about it, and Grey observed it was mostly those people who had already elected to stay in the game. The ones who enjoyed being in virtual reality.

The people fighting to get home didn't seem to care much. Grey was interested, but only because it meant more changes to adapt to. He was just getting used to the game and the map, and here it kept changing. He didn't want to recall all the patches—he wanted to get home before whatever that rocket launch would bring.

"There have been three bug reports registered for investigation," the Admin continued. "Thank you for your observations. We will review these overnight and inform you of any changes made in the morning before the day's battles. The practice area has now been updated with the patch's altered equipment. You have the customary three hours to take advantage of that resource. This concludes Day Thirty of Battles."

When the Admin disappeared, people rushed for the practice zone. Up until now, they had been using the old weapons and only preparing in theory. But now everyone was eager to see just how the changes impacted their play.

Grey dragged his feet.

Kiri stuck by him, not speaking, but he still felt exposed. It felt like everyone was looking at him, and not out of admiration but out of pity. He didn't know what he'd do if Ben or Tristan tried to talk to him. He still didn't want to hear their excuses.

"We'll take you, Kiri, if you're looking!" Sandhya called as she passed. "Or Grey! Are you guys staying together?"

Grey could hardly believe Hazel's old squad was so eager when they had spent half the season trolling them. He could see them stealing his strategies and dumping him just like his supposed "friends."

"We'd like to stick together," Kiri said. "Thanks, though."

Sandhya shrugged. "Let us know if you change your mind."

"Sure," Kiri said.

It wasn't more than five seconds before Robert, the older man who had been sucked into the game at the same time as Grey and Kiri, came up to them. "I'd love to be in your squad, if you'd take a player like me. I know I'm not great, but you kids could teach me a thing or two. I know it."

Grey felt a twinge of sympathy for the guy. At least he was new like them, even if he wanted to use them in the end.

"Sorry, we're not looking to fill the squad right

away. We're trying to think things through," Kiri said. "We'll let you know."

"Fair enough." The guy looked sad but not surprised. "Sorry about your split. This game isn't very nice, is it?"

"Yeah . . ." Kiri said as they slowly walked out of the battle warehouse.

"Hard lessons for all of us new people," Robert said with a sigh. "Never felt so out of place in my life, and I've lived longer than all of you. I'm sure of it."

Grey felt a pang of guilt, but he still kept his mouth shut. He didn't want to talk to anyone. And he didn't want to be swayed by his emotions. He had heard Hazel lying just last night in her attempts to persuade Tae Min. Ben and Tristan had pretended to be his friends only to leave him behind. He wasn't about to trust anyone new today. Or maybe ever again.

"Well, good luck, kids," Robert said as he walked toward the practice area.

Now it was just Kiri and Grey. They stood by the cabins, but Grey could already tell that several people were waiting for them in the practice area. While he wanted to use the patched weapons to practice, that would mean more talks like this. And who would they practice with now? Clearly everyone they had been working with was in on this betrayal.

"We can't avoid everyone forever," Kiri said.

"I know." Grey shoved his hands in his pockets. "I just . . . ugh, I don't want to *see* them or *talk* to them. If I could practice without that, I could do it."

"Okay, I can work with that," Kiri said. "I'll grab the new stuff. We can go farther out in the practice area like we used to. Somewhere no one will bother us, ay?"

Grey nodded. "Thanks. Sorry I suck."

"You don't suck." Kiri punched his shoulder. "All of this sucks. Meet at the outhouse?"

"Sure."

While Kiri ran off to the practice warehouse, Grey went around. He was still able to enter the practice area, but he steered clear of the warehouse and the field where most people practiced their building. Instead, he headed for their old favorite place just outside of the ghost town. He didn't like being there, since it brought up memories of when he first got recruited by Ben, but it was quiet at least.

After a few minutes of waiting, Grey heard

footsteps and turned to greet Kiri. But instead he was met with a person he never expected to face: Hazel.

"Hey, Pip-squeak," she said.

But it didn't have the same bite as usual. He couldn't quite believe it, but Hazel didn't stand in her super-confident way. She had her arms folded over her chest, and she hardly looked him in the eye.

He already had a feeling he knew what she was about to ask, and he couldn't believe it. "What do you want, Hazel?"

She shrugged. "You have a squad. I need a squad. Thought we could work out a deal."

Grey just stood there, unable to process how she could have the gall to ask after how mean she'd been. All the anger he'd held inside throughout the day threatened to break through, and because it was Hazel, he let it.

CHAPTER 6

"Seriously? After all the things you've said about me and Kiri?" Grey scoffed at Hazel. "You want to be in our squad? I can't believe you would even think I'd say yes. You're a total troll, and you didn't even change when your own squad kicked you out."

Hazel let out an angry grunt. "Why do I have to be *nice*? What has being nice gotten you? Has it gotten you into a top-ten squad? No! It got you played by Ben and Tristan. I'm not here to pretend I'm nice—I'm a good player. I've mostly kept my rank up even solo. You can't deny I can offer you something."

Grey narrowed his eyes. She wasn't necessarily

wrong, and at this point part of him appreciated her harsh honesty. "You're really convincing me."

"Stop being so sentimental," Hazel said with an eye roll. "You want to get home. I want to get home. The veteran players are obviously shutting us out whether we're good players or not. We should team up and teach them all a lesson. Why waste your time sulking when you can get revenge?"

Revenge. Did Grey even want revenge?

He was mad. Hurt. But he wasn't sure revenge would make him feel better. He didn't want to stop Ben and Tristan from getting home because of what they did . . . but he didn't want to stay here because of them, either.

"Hazel?" Kiri's voice cut through the quiet. Understanding crossed her face, and she let out a short laugh. "You have *got* to be kidding me. You are not asking to join us."

"She is," Grey said.

"Why is that so hard to comprehend?" Hazel asked. "Is it 'cause you're both little kids?"

Kiri glared at her. "So charming."

"I don't need to be charming to eliminate people in-game!" Hazel yelled. "Why does everyone want me to be nice? I am only saying what everyone else wants to say but won't. Aren't you tired of these stupid games?"

Grey *was* tired. But that didn't mean he wanted to deal with Hazel. "Fine, how about you try out, then? We reserve the right to decide."

Hazel raised an eyebrow. "You want me to audition for you? Like I haven't already proven myself?"

"If you can't even do that," Grey said, "you won't listen to me in battles. How am I supposed to be the leader if you won't listen?"

Hazel scrunched up her face. Grey was sure she'd stomp off and that would be the end of it, but then she said, "Fine. What do you want me to do?"

"Let's check out your aim first," Grey said.

"Wait," Kiri said with horror. "Are you serious? I don't want to play with her."

"It's just an audition," Grey said. "We don't have to accept her."

Kiri glared at Hazel. "I don't know about this, mate."

"I won't squad anyone you don't agree with," Grey asserted. "But she wants a chance, so we may as well so she'll stop bothering us. We can do this with others too, ay?"

"'Ay?' I'm rubbing off on you," Kiri said. "All right, audition away."

Grey didn't know exactly how to make Hazel try out, but since he wasn't taking it seriously, he made stuff up. He honestly didn't have any intention of putting her in his squad.

And it was an opportunity to mess with her.

First, he tested her sniper range by building several towers for them to stand in. He then tasked Hazel with having to hit them within two, five, and ten seconds. She wasn't very good at it, and he enjoyed watching her get frustrated. Then he had her try to hit them as they were rushing the towers. Hazel was slightly better at that but not nearly as good as Kiri.

After that, he tested her at closer range by moving into the ghost town and playing hide-and-seek. Hazel was much better at this, able to dodge and take accurate shots while jumping or moving behind walls to protect herself. Her fear-lessness worked well for her in these situations.

Grey hated to admit this was a skill Ben and Tristan had brought—and Hazel would make a decent replacement. Maybe a better one, if she'd take a few tips.

Next it was time to test her building. He

already knew she had the speed, so he decided they would duel. "Let's do a build battle. You versus me."

"Bring it on," Hazel replied.

"Only wood. No bouncers or traps," Grey said, since he hadn't grabbed any at the practice warehouse. They now stood on a hill far from the main practice area. "First to five hits wins."

"Tell me when," Hazel said as she backed up about twenty yards.

Kiri moved so that she stood right between them, holding up her hand. "Three . . . two . . . one . . . go!"

Hazel used a ramp first, which Grey had expected. He used a floor tile to build on to her ramp and ran underneath it. Quickly, he edited the floor to open a hole and shot up. Hazel's body blinked red.

"One!" Grey called as he closed the floor with editing. Hazel jumped down, probably determined not to fall for that again. Grey had fully boxed himself into the structure.

As she shot to break one wall, Grey edited another and built two ramps to get the high ground. He turned and switched to his shotgun, taking two more shots on her.

"Ugh!" Hazel cried. She shot back, but he had already put up a wall to block it.

Grey smiled, not realizing he'd gotten this much better at building than Hazel. She had clearly been relying on her old squad for their building skill, though she never would admit that to anyone. He built up just one more ramp to peek over his wall and got Hazel two more times without even getting hit. "And five. I win."

Hazel shook her head, looking as sore of a loser as ever. "How'd you do that, Pip-squeak?"

Grey shrugged. "Practice."

"Lots of people practice and don't figure out how to build like that," Hazel said as she looked over the SMG she held.

Grey had a feeling she meant herself, not that he'd point it out. "Well, that's the end of your audition."

"And?" Hazel asked.

Grey and Kiri glanced at each other, and then Kiri said, "We'll let you know. We both agreed we weren't rushing to fill the squad."

"It's not like you have all season," Hazel pointed out. "But okay."

"One more question," Grey said. He couldn't help but mention it now that he had the upper hand. "I heard you talking to Tae Min last night. You lied about wanting to go home because your dad was dying. What's the real reason?"

Hazel raised an eyebrow. "Eavesdropping, huh? Here I thought you were squeaky clean."

"You'd lie about that?" Kiri put her hands on her hips. "How can we trust you if we don't even know why you want to get home? You seem to like this game a lot—why not just stay?"

Some of the fight left Hazel as she let out a sigh. She wouldn't look at either of them as she spoke. "I would stay, totally, but I don't think I have that kind of time, you know?"

Grey wasn't quite following, and he hated to admit it. "I don't get it."

"People don't like me, okay? Not just in this game, but in real life, too. I . . . I don't have anyone out there worried I'm in a coma." Hazel glared at the ground. "I ran away from home in high school. All I have is me, my crappy job, and a cat. If I'm in a coma out there in the real world . . . I don't know how long I've got until the doctors pull the plug because there's no one to pay the bill. So, yeah, I'd love to stay in this game, but I also don't want to die for real."

Hazel walked away after that, leaving Grey

and Kiri to watch and wonder. "Do you think that was the truth, Kiri?"

"I have no idea . . ." Kiri had fear in her eyes as she looked at Grey. "Would the doctors do that? The Admin said no one had died in real life while playing."

"That doesn't mean it can't happen, though." Grey felt a chill of fear run through him. While he wasn't immediately afraid that his parents would give up on him being stuck in a coma, how long would it take? Some people were already giving up for the season, deciding to stay instead. Were they from families they knew would keep them alive in the real world? How many in the top twenty were fighting because they were afraid they only had so long in the real world before people gave up on them?

For a brief moment, he wasn't so mad at Ben and Tristan anymore. They'd never said what Hazel just had, but it must have crossed their minds in the eleven months they'd been stuck in the game.

If Grey had been stuck there for a year, maybe he wouldn't care so much about friends as he would about making it out of this game alive. Was that why the veterans began to stick together? They knew that fear. They had less time to gamble than Grey or Kiri did.

"What's wrong, Grey?" Kiri asked.

He shook his head. "Nothing. Just not so mad at Ben and Tristan suddenly."

Kiri nodded. "Yeah, seriously. They must be thinking the same thing as Hazel."

"Just wish they'd told us that." Grey began walking back toward the practice warehouse, suddenly not in the mood to keep doing drills. "I never really thought about dying for real."

Kiri walked beside him. "Yeah, me either. My parents wouldn't give up on me. I know that for sure."

"Me too." The more Grey thought about it, the less angry he became. He was still sad that Ben and Tristan didn't warn him, but he could say at that moment he wanted them to make it home more than he wanted to go home. They had lived with that fear for who knew how long, and that wasn't fair for anyone to face.

CHAPTER 7

The next morning, Grey could tell Ben wanted to say something to him. Grey waited because he wasn't sure what to say either. He wasn't nearly as mad as before, but he wasn't about to forgive them either. Grey had to move on because he still wanted to make it home this season, even if other people thought he was too new to deserve it.

"You know we couldn't pass up Zach's squad, right?" Ben finally said.

"I know," Grey replied without looking at him. He wished he had something to do, but there were no clothes to change into. No food to eat or showers to take before the day's battles. No excuses to escape a conversation he didn't want to have.

"We couldn't tell you," Tristan continued. "It's a compliment. You're too good and we needed an advantage to distance our ranks."

Grey tried to remain as stoic as Tae Min, though he wanted to scoff at Tristan's attempt at making this sound like a flattering move. "Good luck. I hope you get home."

"Dang, is he made of steel now?" Lorenzo asked as Grey walked out of the cabin without even a glance backward.

Grey was on the lookout for Kiri. They had been so preoccupied thinking about Ben and Tristan last night that they never discussed whether or not to consider Hazel's petition to be on their squad. Of the people who had asked to join them—many more than Grey could have guessed—she had been the best. Everyone else was much lower ranked.

But there was still an issue with her attitude. And the fact that they both didn't like her.

Kiri was outside her cabin, and there were several lower-ranked players talking to her. Probably trying to sell themselves as candidates for their squad. When she spotted Grey, she ran over. "There you are! Let's talk strategy before the day starts."

"Yeah, sure," Grey said as she pulled him away from all the people.

"They are going to drive me mad," Kiri whispered. "We need to fill the squad just so people will stop asking."

"We never talked about Hazel," Grey said. "I wanted to ask what you think."

Kiri cringed. "I still don't know. She has a good rank even solo, and her skills are similar to the ones we lost, but . . ."

"It's still Hazel?"

"Exactly."

They had walked to the battle warehouse, and though they still had time before battles started, there were other groups huddled around talking strategy as well. No one spoke above a whisper, and it reminded Grey of a library.

"If she would agree to listen . . ." Grey continued. "I don't know. I can't deny she's got potential. Her building is weak, but not impossible to fix."

"And she's new like us," Kiri pointed out. "Which seems important all of a sudden."

"Yeah, the veterans might ditch us." Grey sighed. "You okay trying another day as duo? I still don't think I'm ready to squad up with anyone."

Kiri nodded. "Yeah. We can figure it out. No worries."

But Grey was worried. Each day as a duo felt like a day they would lose more rank. And if they wanted to make it home this season, dropping in rank was not the way to go. Though what else could they do? The veterans were determined to stop them. "We just gotta stay in the top thirties, even if we have to hide like cowards to do it."

"I'm good with that."

"Cool." Grey knew everyone looked down on turtling and hiding—even he had at times—but this was all they could do until they made a decision on squad members or figured out how to be overpowering as a duo.

The day's battles began, and they went about as Grey expected them to go. He and Kiri struggled to stay in the top thirty, and their ranking inched down at each game they had. They hadn't done horribly, but it didn't feel like they were doing well either. To Grey, it felt like he was going nowhere.

Over the next several days, they landed in places that weren't as populated, waiting out the early fights and storms until they were at least in the top forty. Their fights went okay—sometimes they ranked into the twenties—but whenever they found a full squad, things would go sour quickly.

"We need to make a decision on squad members," Kiri said as they were eliminated in their last battle on the third day. This time at ranks thirty-one and thirty. "We can't stand up to top-tier firepower."

Grey sighed as he switched to watch Tae Min while they waited for the battle to be over. "How does Tae Min do it solo? I just don't get it."

"He's not human, I swear," Kiri said. "Or he must have already been pro level before he got sucked in here."

"Maybe." While Grey had learned a little bit about Tae Min, he still didn't know his gaming background. "He can't be done with high school, though."

"Doesn't mean he's not pro level," Kiri insisted.

Tae Min still won at least two games a day, usually more. And Grey actually enjoyed watching him take out all the people who had decided to cut him and Kiri out of the race for top five.

"So," Grey said as Tae Min took out Hans's

squad with some C4 and several perfect shots. "Hazel's still the best who's tried out for us."

"Yeah . . ." Kiri admitted, though she sounded reluctant. They had auditioned a handful of other players that were ranked in the forties and thirties, and none of them had quite stood up to Hazel's skill in close range, which was something they needed. "I can't believe I'm saying this, but she's the only one that stands out at all."

"I guess we have to suck it up and offer her a spot then," Grey said. "Because we're not getting far enough, fast enough on our own."

"Okay, after this," Kiri replied.

The battle ended, and everyone appeared in their ranked line for the day as usual. Grey and Kiri stood right by Hazel as if it was some kind of destiny, also showing how far they'd dropped in just a few days. They'd have to fight for a lot of wins if they had any chance at getting into the top five.

The Admin appeared, and for once she didn't wear her usual smile. The serious expression made Grey nervous before she even spoke. "I regret to announce that Robert has died in the real world and thus has been removed from the competition."

Gasps and cries of shock filled the warehouse. Grey could hardly believe what he was hearing. Robert was dead? Real dead. He'd only been here as long as Grey had . . . and now he was gone. Forever. He was older—had he been sick in the real world already? Or had his family decided he wasn't coming back from the coma? Either way, Grey was scared. It sounded like everyone was scared.

"No, no, no . . ." Hazel, who stood next to Grey, covered her mouth and squeezed her eyes shut. She started to shake. "I knew it. I knew I was doomed."

"Please calm down." The Admin's voice grew louder. "Allow me to speak!"

The room went silent.

"Thank you." The Admin straightened her suit coat. "I know this is concerning. And we deeply regret that this has happened. Robert had been ill prior to his arrival in the game, and we did not predict how a coma would impact his issues. It was an oversight that will be corrected in future selections for this virtual reality battleground.

"Because of this, we will enact a previously unused measure to keep the battle at one hundred players. A new player will be invited immediately, but because of the mid-season nature of the invitation, they will be granted a ranking of fifty instead of one hundred upon entry. We feel this is fair to everyone. Please welcome this new player right now."

The Admin held out her hand, and a person began to appear. Grey's eyes went wide as he took the new player in. Not because it was shocking to see or because of the unexpected news—but because Grey actually recognized the head of curly red hair and the face full of freckles.

The new player was Finn, Grey's best friend in real life.

CHAPTER 8

Grey stood there, as shocked as he had been the first day he arrived. Finn looked around in a daze, probably trying to figure out what just happened. Grey remembered that feeling all too well. Except he hadn't arrived alone like Finn.

Though Finn wasn't technically by himself—what with Grey being there.

Would Kiri be okay recruiting Finn to their squad? Grey had to. Finn already knew the game. He was good at it. They were best friends.

Maybe he and Kiri wouldn't be doomed after all.

The Admin popped up in front of Finn, and he jumped in surprise. "Dude! What the crap?"

"Greetings, new player!" the Admin said with

a smile, already having moved on completely from Robert's death like it was nothing. She had to be a computer program, Grey decided right then—no human could do that. He was still reeling, and he hardly knew the guy. "Welcome to the competition of a lifetime! You have been randomly selected for this special, virtual reality edition of Fortnite Battle Royale. I am the Admin and will be facilitating your tutorial . . ."

The Admin went on just like she had when Grey first arrived. It was strange to watch, being on the other side of the audience. Finn hadn't caught sight of Grey yet, and Grey wasn't sure if he should wave or wait until the Admin had finished her speech.

But just as the Admin started in on the rules, Finn's vision drifted to the people behind him. His eyes found Grey within seconds, and recognition hit. Finn lifted his finger and pointed. "Grey! You're *here*?"

Now everyone's eyes were on Grey, even the Admin's. Grey nodded. "Hey, Finn. Sorry you're stuck here, but good to see you."

"Everyone was so freaked out the day you collapsed!" Finn said. "So that just happened to me, too?"

"Yeah." Grey gulped, never imagining he'd get to hear about what happened *after* he got stuck in Battle Royale. "Is my family . . . all right?"

Finn cringed. "They're pretty stressed. No one knows what's wrong with you. But you're here. Crazy."

"Excuse me," the Admin cut in. "Grey, will you please divulge how you are acquainted with the new player?"

"He's my friend," Grey said. "We go to school together."

"I need to speak with my superiors about this development. We have never had two players know each other in the real world before," the Admin said and then disappeared.

The room erupted in discussion the moment she was gone. People weren't just talking about Robert dying, but the idea that Grey and Finn knew each other. Was that fair? Would that be a security risk to whomever was running this hacked version of Fortnite Battle Royale? Grey didn't care about any of that right now. He ran over to Finn. He would have hugged him, but he figured that would look suspicious.

"Are you okay?" Grey asked.

Finn looked around, smiling a little. "I mean, this is like Fortnite, but for real, yeah?"

"Pretty much," Grey said. "A few things might be different. I don't know. I was just about to play for the first time when I collapsed, remember?"

"Right." Finn's smile grew bigger. "Well, I'm pumped then! Now my mom can't tell me to stop playing. I have to play!"

Grey was hardly surprised at Finn's excitement. Finn had been obsessed with the game before Grey got stuck. Obviously that hadn't changed in the month Grey had been gone. "It's basically all we can do. No food. No TV. Nothing but Fortnite and a forced resting period."

"It's like a dream," Finn said. "Are you sure it's not a dream?"

"No dream of mine," Kiri's voice said from behind. Grey turned to find her standing there eyeing Finn. "Is your friend any good, Grey?"

"He was the one who was supposed to teach me before I got stuck here," Grey said. "Finn, this is my squad mate, Kiri. She's an amazing sniper."

"Oh yeah? Well, I've killed streamers," Finn bragged. "I'm gonna be a pro when I'm old enough."

"Aren't you flash." Kiri smiled, though Grey

knew by now that her statement wasn't so much a compliment as it was sarcasm. "Guess we found our fourth squad member, ay?"

"If you're okay with that . . ." Grey gulped, not wanting to upset Kiri. "We pick together, right?"

"Wouldn't hurt if you can vouch for him," Kiri said.

"I can." Grey looked at Finn. "You wanna be in our squad?"

Finn smiled wide and placed his hand on Grey's shoulder. "Dude, of course! Why would I pick anyone else?"

Grey shrugged. Honestly, it was a relief that Finn was still his friend. Grey hadn't realized it, but part of him had wondered if people had begun to forget about him in the real world. The longer he spent trapped in the game, the more it felt like his reality was a dream. But having Finn here now reminded him what he was fighting for—he was fighting to get that real life back.

And now he had a real friend to help him get it.

It had to have been sheer luck, based on the Admin's surprise. But after everything that had happened with Ben and Tristan, Grey would take any speck of luck he could get.

"We still adding Hazel?" Kiri asked.

Grey nodded. "I think we should."

"I'll go get her." Kiri walked off.

"Who's Hazel?" Finn asked.

"Someone who wanted to be in our squad," Grey said as he looked around the room. A lot of people were still stealing glances at them, but they had mostly turned to talking among themselves. No one had left yet—the Admin hadn't technically ended the day like usual. Nothing about the end of this day was usual, not even for whoever ran this game. "You see, we had two guys ditch us for a higher-ranked squad a few days ago, so we've had people wanting to fill those spots."

"Seriously?" Finn raised one of his carrot-colored eyebrows.

Grey nodded. "It's pretty normal, I guess. Lots of people vying for those top five spots to get home."

"Who was it?" Finn asked as he scanned the room.

"Over there, the two blond guys about our age," Grey said as he glanced at Ben and Tristan.

"Jerks." Finn glared at them, and they definitely noticed. "I'll avenge you."

Grey felt bad. That wasn't what he'd intended, though he appreciated Finn's loyalty. "They helped me out when I first got here. It's not that simple. They've been in the game for almost a year. At some point you just really want to go home, you know?"

Finn didn't look like he understood at all. "Why would you want to go home? We're inside a video game! What could be better?"

"Now this is a cool kid," Hazel said as she and Kiri came back to join them. "Finn, was it?"

"Yeah, and you're Hazel?" Finn asked.

"Yup." She looked between them all, hesitating for a moment before she said, "Does this mean I'm in the squad finally?"

"Only if you can listen to Grey," Kiri said. "And work on your building. And not be a total jerk all the time."

Hazel sighed. "I guess I can do that, but I reserve the right to be a jerk at least half the time. It's sort of my thing."

"I just need you to take advice, in and out of game," Grey said. "You act like you're all that, but you have weaknesses we need to fix if we want victories. Once we get those, you can brag all you want."

While Hazel didn't seem totally on board, she still nodded. "It's a deal."

"Okay," Grey said. "I'll send the invites then."

"You're the leader, huh?" Finn said, surprised. "Who convinced you to do that?"

"Mostly me," Kiri said. "He's got a knack for it."

"He sure does," Finn said. "He just never had the confidence to actually do it. You must be pretty persuasive."

"She is," Grey said as he sent out the invites from the menu that he could access as a squad leader. They accepted the invite immediately. And now Grey once again had a full squad to work with. While he wasn't entirely sure how it would go, he still liked knowing he had the extra help. Even being a duo for a few days had hurt his rankings enough that it would take a miracle to make top five before the end of the season.

The Admin appeared again, and everyone quieted down. She wore the usual fake smile, so Grey figured the news wouldn't be too bad. "After reviewing what we know of Grey and Finn's relationship in the real world, we have determined to allow the selection to play out as is. Finn will remain in the game in place of Robert until he ranks in the top five at the end of the season. All rules will apply to him as they apply to everyone, save his rank being modified to fifty instead of starting out at one hundred."

"I can accept that," Finn said. "When do I get to play?"

"Your positive attitude is welcome," the Admin said. "This concludes Day Thirty-Four of Battles. You may try the battle format in the practice area. I assume Grey will show you around, since you are close already. Tomorrow's battles will begin after mandatory rest. Finn, your cabin is posted next to the rankings on the wall. Good luck, everyone."

The Admin disappeared, leaving everyone to the usual practice time after fights. Finn was excited to get out there, and as they showed him the warehouse and practice area, he bounced around like a kid who just got the best birthday present ever.

"This is awesome!" he cried as he looked over the wall of weapons and pulled out all the legendary ones. "It's like playground mode but better because everything is here to test without searching the map for it!"

"Playground mode?" Hazel said. "I don't remember that."

"It just came out like two weeks ago," Finn said.

"Ah, got it." Hazel looked disappointed. "So we are missing more new stuff from the actual game."

"Maybe?" Finn grabbed the materials with wonder. "Whoa, infinity mats? Nice! Do you guys have shopping carts?"

Grey raised an eyebrow. "Shopping carts?"

Finn nodded. "Yeah, that you can push around. Or you can get in while a buddy pushes you. It's hilarious."

"Never seen one in here," Kiri said.

"They don't have hop rocks, either," Hazel said. "I miss those."

"Really?" Finn looked surprised. "Weird. Wonder why not."

Grey remembered watching Finn use hop rocks to bounce and move extra far. It was only another reminder that this virtual reality wasn't quite like the actual game. "Sounds like it could be movement related?"

"Did the rocket show up?" Finn asked. "Everyone is freaking out about the rocket."

"Yeah, we got that, but not so much the freaking out," Kiri said. "Some of the people who have decided to stay are excited about it. But those of us fighting to get home don't care."

Finn nodded. "Makes sense."

"We better get in some practice," Grey said as he grabbed an SMG, a shotgun, and some explosives. "They just nerfed ARs and materials in llamas here, Finn. Any reports on the real-world changes?"

"We got those recently, too," he said. "SMGs and shotguns are way in. I've practiced with them."

"Nice." As Grey looked at his squad, it felt weird to see new faces. He grew nervous about his ability to lead a different combination of people. He wasn't worried about Hazel's or Finn's ability, but he still didn't know how they would fit in to what he'd already done as a leader. That was what he'd have to figure out, and he needed to do it fast.

CHAPTER 9

Grey knew what his squad needed for practice, but he was terrified to make it happen. As he exited the practice warehouse, he looked around at all the people building. Grey's squad needed to scrimmage against one of these teams. He couldn't ask Hans's squad after knowing they were in on the betrayal. And there was no way he'd ask Zach's squad either.

He would have to ask someone else. Someone he didn't know as well. Someone who was probably lower ranked than him.

"What's up?" Kiri asked.

"We need to practice against someone. I know they're good, but we have to work on team play," Grey said.

"Ah, yeah." Kiri winced. "Who to ask?"

"That's the question . . ." Hazel's old squad was about the same rank, but that wouldn't work because they didn't like her. There were several people he recognized, but he hadn't paid attention to who they were exactly. Half the people stuck there weren't even practicing at this point, having resigned to staying in the game. They would have dance parties by the cabins, using their earned dance moves and emotes from the game.

Grey spotted Lorenzo, another player who had arrived that season with Grey. He was a big, semi-troll of a football player, but he and his team had stuck in the thirties and forties for the better part of the season. They were just behind Hazel's old squad, for the most part.

Lorenzo hadn't been super nice to Grey, but he hadn't betrayed him, either. Plus he was new, so maybe he'd be open to helping other new players, unlike the veterans.

Grey took a deep breath. "What about Lorenzo's squad?"

Kiri looked open to it, but before she could answer, Hazel jumped in.

"Lorenzo sucks!" Hazel said with a sneer.

"You already know we can beat them. How is that practice?"

"I don't know that," Grey said in frustration. "Remember how you're not in charge?"

Hazel scrunched her lips together. "I forgot."

"Maybe we were better than them before," Grey said. "But I have no clue what kind of synergy we have now. And I don't want to show our moves to all the people who just betrayed us."

"Fair enough," Hazel said.

Now Grey had to go up and actually ask Lorenzo, which was the most nerve-wracking part. He hated asking for things, and he worried Lorenzo would say no. Grey walked up to the large tower where Lorenzo's squad shot at each other from different perches. The practice method was too static, from Grey's experience. He'd learned his squad improved faster when they were forced to be on the move constantly.

Grey took a couple shots, and he looked up to find Lorenzo. The guy yelled, "Well, well, what're you doing under my tower?"

"Just wondering if your squad is interested in practicing with mine." Grey called back. "What do you think?"

"One sec! Lemme discuss it with everyone."

Lorenzo disappeared into the tower, as did the rest of the people on his squad.

It felt like ages for Lorenzo and his squad to appear from the door in the bottom of their tower. Lorenzo wore a smug grin as he eyed Grey, as if he had the advantage even though his squad would benefit a lot from practicing with Grey's, too. The others with Lorenzo were people Grey only knew by name—Coco, Julio, and Selena. They were all similar ages, older teens or early twenties, but he didn't know where they were from or anything about their real lives.

"We talked it over," Lorenzo said. "And everyone thinks it's a good idea to learn from you guys. So don't hold back, okay?"

"Sure thing," Grey said with a smile. He looked back at the other teams practicing in the area. Ben and Tristan were definitely paying attention, and Grey didn't like that. "You mind moving to a more remote location? I don't want our competition spying."

"Fine by me." Lorenzo looked up at Tristan and Ben on their looming sky base. He leaned in to whisper to Grey. "People are saying they dropped your squad right before a battle with no word. That true?"

Grey nodded.

Lorenzo winced. "Heartless, man. I thought y'all were tight."

"Turns out veterans stick together," Grey said. "Maybe us new people should, too."

"Yeah, man." Lorenzo held up a hand for a high five. Grey slapped his palm, and Lorenzo grabbed it into a handshake. "We won't ice you like that. Not gonna lie, we want to learn from your building skills."

"I can accept that." Right now, Grey appreciated people who were at least open about their motivations. If someone wanted to benefit from Grey's abilities, he'd rather they just say it out loud. "Let's work down by the river, if that's okay."

"We'll load up on weapons and meet you there," Lorenzo replied.

Grey ran back to his squad. They were over by the targets practicing shots. Finn looked stressed. "Ugh! It shouldn't be this different from the actual game!"

"You'll get it," Kiri said. "You've already gotten better."

"Not having the crosshair bites," Hazel said.

"Lorenzo's group is in," Grey announced. "They're meeting us by the river."

"Sweet as, mate!" Kiri reloaded her sniper. "Let's see what we can do, ay?"

"We're gonna wreck them," Hazel said with a smile. One that actually seemed genuine. So far, she didn't seem that bad, but maybe she was trying to play nice. If she really was afraid of dying in the real world, then Robert's death must have shaken her to the core.

"I can't wait," Finn said as he bounced up and down.

Grey couldn't help but smile. His friend was just as excited to be here as Grey imagined, and it brought a welcome jolt of energy to Grey to have someone around who actually wanted to experience this virtual reality. Maybe Finn didn't quite understand what it would mean to be stuck here for months, but they'd face that when it hit.

The river was an out-of-the-way place in the practice area. There was a cave here that Grey and his squad had used to hide from Hazel a few times. Grey decided to keep that spot secret from Hazel still. Just in case.

There was a part where the river widened and a bridge stretched over its banks. Grey stopped there to wait for Lorenzo's squad. They showed up within a few minutes, and Lorenzo smiled. "All ready for us, huh?"

"Yup!" Hazel said as she pulled out a minigun and mowed them over with shots. They all just stood there, blinking red but not taking damage. "Gotcha! Game over."

"Funny," Lorenzo said as they met Grey's squad on the bridge. "So how do you want to do this, Grey? Rumor has it you're the practice god."

"I am?" Grey had never heard this rumor.

"Yeah," Selena, a girl with super-curly brown hair, chimed in. "Everyone says you made Ben and Tristan what they are now. They sucked before."

"Now I can't beat them," Julio, the guy with the buzz cut, said. "How'd you do that?"

Grey shrugged. He hadn't thought about how he'd helped Ben and Tristan improve, though he did know they'd gotten a lot better. "How about squad-vs-squad build battles? That's what we need to work on. Five hits and the squad member is downed, two more and eliminated. First to eliminate the other team wins."

"Sounds good to me," Lorenzo said. "Take opposite sides of the bridge?"

"Yeah. You call start." Grey moved back to the far side of the bridge, while Lorenzo's team went to the side closer to the practice warehouse.

Lorenzo held up one of his muscled arms. "In three . . . two . . . one!"

Before a single wall went up, Finn lobbed several grenades at the opposing team. They scattered to avoid getting hit. Grey was surprised, but he began to build up ramps for higher ground. "Building up, Finn. Follow me!"

"But they're sitting ducks!" Finn was already building out his own side. "Gonna flank!"

"Uhhh . . ." Grey wasn't prepared for how aggressive Finn would be, but he decided to see how it would play out. Finn placed a bounce pad on a wall, and he used it to fly over Lorenzo's team and onto the hill behind them.

"Watch out!" Coco cried as she shot at Finn.

Lorenzo's squad was already frantically boxing themselves in rather than building up to fight. Grey wasn't sure if that was because the grenades threw them off or they defaulted to defense rather than offense.

Finn opened up with his SMG, mowing down Lorenzo's squad's walls so they couldn't get a leg up. Coco was already downed, and Grey knew all he had to do was throw a couple C4 and they'd be done for.

"Following Finn! That looks fun!" Hazel said as she ran for the bounce pad and flew to the other side. Adding her minigun fire to Finn's SMG, it was impossible for Lorenzo's squad to keep the walls up.

"This just doesn't feel fair . . ." Kiri said as she and Grey just stood there watching.

"Not at all." And it wasn't because Grey thought his squad was better. He marched out to the bridge, waving his hands. "Hold up! Hold up! Cease fire!"

Everyone stopped fighting.

"We almost had them all!" Finn said.

"I know," Grey said. "But this isn't the kind of practice I'm looking for. I want to see *building* practice. How about we start over with a no explosives rule?"

"Yes, please." Lorenzo glared up at Finn. "We didn't expect grenades—we expected ramps and walls. I didn't stock up on that stuff."

"You gotta be ready for everything!" Hazel called back.

Finn laughed. "Yeah!"

Grey's stomach twisted. He was already

starting to see the problems their squad could have. Namely, Finn already had trolling tendencies, and Hazel could easily bring those out in him. Those two combined might be hard for Grey to rein in.

Finn also knew how Grey was in real life. Quiet. A follower. Not a leader. Would he listen to Grey?

Grey straightened, trying to embrace the role he'd grown more comfortable with. "Right, you gotta be ready for everything—including when you have no explosives to rely on as a crutch. They're powerful, but they run out fast even if you do get them. So right now we're working on *building*. Not exploding. Anyone can do that."

Finn and Hazel stared at him in shock. Neither of them had heard him be assertive, and for a moment Grey was certain they'd both walk away.

"Okay," Finn finally said. "Building, it is."

"Let's start over then," Grey said. He turned to Lorenzo. "Sorry about that."

"No worries. Thanks for being fair," Lorenzo replied. "I appreciate that. You're cooler than I thought."

"Thanks . . . I think." Grey went back over

the bridge, destroying the walls and ramps he'd made as they went so it would be a fresh battlefield.

"Good job," Kiri said when they met up. "It won't be easy to rein them in, will it?"

Grey sighed. "I doubt it."

Finn and Hazel came back to their side, both quiet like they just got scolded by a teacher. It made Grey feel uncomfortable. Up until now, he'd mostly had to encourage his squad mates and they listened to him before they did anything too crazy. They would at least ask if Grey wanted a flank before doing it.

But Finn was used to playing solo. He probably assumed he was better than all of them. Maybe he was. But if they couldn't play as a team . . . none of this would go well.

CHAPTER 10

Practice went a little better after that, but Grey still felt like he was on shaky ground with his new squad mates. It felt strange to boss around Finn and Hazel, and the way they looked at him when he said things made it clear they found it weird, too. He could feel their resistance, something he'd never had to worry about with Ben and Tristan. They had just absorbed all his suggestions like sponges.

But Hazel and Finn had never played in his squad. They hadn't seen how his leadership improved their success. Both were obviously still skeptical of his abilities, even if other people weren't.

They were now in the middle of their fifth skirmish against Lorenzo's team and Grey had been hit three times. Kiri was pretend-eliminated. Finn and Hazel weren't much safer than Grey. Lorenzo's team had started out weak, but the practice had clearly helped them figure out some better tactics as well. That was the risk with practicing against competition. Grey didn't like that part, but he did like that he was able to see where Finn and Hazel stood on their building skills.

Finn was great, though a little more aggressive than he needed to be. It was clear he'd played a lot of solo battles—he always wanted to do everything himself. Hazel, on the other hand, was more of a defensive builder, always sure to protect herself first and unsure of how to use builds for attacking.

They had a lot of potential to be a great pair.

But right now, they both did the exact opposite things and often blocked each other instead of helping the team.

"Stop ramping up!" Hazel finally yelled as Finn once again fought for high ground. "Getting to max build height isn't going to help!"

"You can't just hide in a box!" Finn called back as he shot at Lorenzo's team below. They were all still standing while Kiri waited from afar for the skirmish to end.

"You're just wasting ammo while they all hide," Hazel replied.

Grey was losing his patience because they were both wrong. He was closer to Hazel, so he'd have to work with her. "Hazel, follow me and keep using those walls to protect us."

"Okay . . ."

Grey began to lay down something both his squad mates seemed to have forgotten existed— floors. While Finn had jumped the gun by flanking on the first battle, right now it was essential for them to get *around* Lorenzo's team. Not above or below. So while they were distracted with Finn's relentless shooting, Grey moved so that he could surround their enemies.

"Ohhh," Hazel said as she realized she had a perfect shot on Coco's back. Which she took without hesitation. "So this is why they put you in the lead."

"Maybe," Grey said as he took several shots on Lorenzo, enough that he raised both hands to indicate he'd been hit enough to be eliminated. Finn took down Julio, and Hazel finished Selena. "It's not about one or the other. You can't keep thinking that the one thing that has worked for you is the only way to build. If you want to win,

I need you to open up and realize it's situational. You have to learn *all* the tactics, not just defensive walls and boxes."

Hazel pursed her lips as she thought. "I'll think about it. Is that it for the day, then?"

"Yeah." It was getting near the time they would all be forced to sleep.

"Tomorrow, then." Hazel walked off without any other comments. Grey figured he'd take that. While she didn't exactly say she'd listen to him, she didn't refuse, either. That was nearly as good as a "Yes, sir" from someone like her.

Lorenzo and his squad met up with Grey on their mess of a tower. Lorenzo wore a big smile. "Nice move, going around while we were distracted. Thanks for the practice. I think we learned a lot."

"I think so, too," Grey said.

"Maybe we could skirmish again sometime?" Lorenzo asked.

Grey nodded. "Sure thing."

As they all jumped down from a height that would normally break bones, Grey sat on the ledge and watched them go. Finn was climbing down to him from above, and it looked like Kiri was already walking back with Lorenzo's squad.

She had an uncanny knack for reading what Grey needed, and right now he needed to talk with Finn one-on-one.

Finn sat next to Grey and dangled his legs in the air. "That was amazing. I can't wait for battles tomorrow. Is the island as awesome as I think it is? I wonder if it's the same as I'm used to."

"I'm not sure, since I never really played outside of here," Grey admitted.

"Oh yeah," Finn said. "We're gonna win every game. We did awesome."

Grey didn't agree. Normally he would go along with Finn, but he couldn't if he wanted to have a fighting chance to get home. "This isn't solos with a bunch of new players, Finn. It's not easy. We probably won't win any of the games. The top twenty here have mostly been around since the first two seasons, fighting every day for their chance to get back to their families and friends. They are hungry and ruthless and dead set on making sure none of us take their spots. I'm glad you're here, and you're an awesome player, but it's not just about your skills solo—it's about teamwork, too."

Finn's red brows cinched over his green eyes. "I know, but we have a good chance. You don't have to be so negative."

"I'm not being negative. I'm being realistic," Grey replied. "I've been here for a month. The game mechanics might be the same as you know, but this world . . . isn't. We fight the same people every day. They learn your style and tactics. They know your weaknesses and exploit them. I need you to *listen* to me and not jump in all the time thinking you know what's best. I know these players more than you do, and I know they will punish you for that over-aggression. Lorenzo's squad is mid-tier. You haven't even seen what the top tier here can do, but I have. I was fighting them, and winning sometimes, before Ben and Tristan moved on."

"You're different here, Grey." Finn looked out at the horizon. Grey couldn't tell if he was mad or not.

"Is that a bad thing?" Grey asked.

"I don't know." Finn gave him a weak smile. "I always pictured me teaching you how to play this game, but here you are teaching me. And you're pretty good, too. It's weird. I can't believe you're a squad leader."

"Me either," Grey admitted. "But it turns out I'm decent at it—if my squad mates will listen to me."

Finn sighed. "Okay, okay. I get it. I'll try. I'm not really used to playing in squads. And not being in charge."

"I know. This is weird for me, too," Grey said. "Actually, when my team was pushing me to lead, I thought about you. Wished you were here instead of me. Sorry if I jinxed you."

"Jinxed?" Finn laughed. "This is a dream come true!"

Five minutes before mandatory bedtime!

"We better go." Grey jumped off the tower, now used to falling and not dying from it.

Finn hesitated for only a moment before he followed. "So weird we can do that and not die."

"Yeah." They walked back to the cabins. Finn was in a different one than Grey, since he'd taken Robert's spot. They waved goodnight, and Grey ran into his cabin right before they had to be in bed.

Hopefully tomorrow would bring more team-work now that Grey had spoken with both Hazel and Finn.

CHAPTER 11

Grey was glad to have practiced with his new team, but he still didn't feel ready for the next day of battles. While they had skills individually, he still didn't know how they fit as a team. And he still wasn't 100 percent sure that Hazel and Finn would listen to him in battle. If they didn't, their ranks would pay for it.

"So . . . everyone's saying you recruited Hazel," Ben said as they all woke up for the day and got out of bed. "Is that true?"

"Maybe." Grey was not in the mood for Ben to make any comments.

Ben gave him a shocked look. "Seriously? Why would you do that when she gave us so much crap?"

Us. Grey had worked hard to keep cool, to

avoid facing Ben and Tristan, but that one word sent him over the edge. "I don't know, maybe because I'm tired of people who pretend to be nice but are really jerks. At least I know what to expect from Hazel."

"He's not wrong," Lorenzo chimed in. "You guys were beyond cold. Legendary cold, not even warning them before you left."

Tristan and Ben looked down, ashamed.

"We need to get home," Tristan said quietly. "You don't understand what it feels like to be here a year."

Lorenzo nodded. "You're right, I don't. But you aren't the only ones who've been here that long—there are lots of people still here from the first season and they aren't betraying their friends."

Grey found it strange that Lorenzo was defending him, but he appreciated it. Now he didn't have to say it himself. "Maybe those people don't want it as badly, Lorenzo."

"Maybe they don't!" Ben replied in frustration. "Lots of people have chosen to stay here because they like it. No one gets crap for giving up the real world, but if you do everything and anything to win, you're the bad guy."

"It's not bad to want to win," Grey said. He didn't want to make anything worse than it already was—he had a new squad to concentrate on. "It's just a shame you didn't think we couldn't do it together. I thought we could. That was always my plan, to help you and Tristan get home."

Ben looked like those words had punched him right in the gut. "Tris, let's go find Zach and Hui Yin."

Once they left, Lorenzo said, "Dang, Grey, you guilt trip better than my mom."

He shrugged. "My mom is the best at it—guess I learned from her."

"Good luck today," Lorenzo said with a smile. "Thanks for the practice. I think my team will rank up today because of you."

"Thanks for helping us out, too," Grey said. "We still have work to do, but we're better prepared for today."

"Try to relax and you'll do fine," he said.

Lorenzo waved as he left the cabin, and now it was just Grey and Tae Min. The top player hadn't gotten up from his bed yet, and Grey hesitated. But he had to ask, "Any tips for getting two overly confident players to listen to me?"

Tae Min grinned ever so slightly. "Don't be soft."

Grey took that in, as simple as it was. He couldn't tiptoe around Finn or Hazel—they would run right over him if he did. He'd have to find the courage to boss them around. "Right, thanks."

"Grey! You still in there?" Kiri called from outside.

"Coming!" Grey hurried outside to find Kiri, Finn, and Hazel. It was a strange sight, even to him, and he could tell everyone else who stared thought the same thing. All new players. A strange mix that didn't quite fit together.

But he would work with what he had.

"Let's talk strategy." He started right in. Because they needed to focus before the day's battles began. "Battle warehouse."

"Yessir!" Finn said with a salute. Grey knew he was trying to listen, but it still felt like he was teasing Grey.

They gathered around a metal picnic table in the battle warehouse. A few other squads had gathered at their own tables for the same discussion. Hans's squad was one of them. And there was a top-twenty duo team as well, Yuri and

Vlad, that kept to themselves much like Tae Min did. Grey could see their serious faces as they spoke, so he knew they would be doing everything in their power to rank well today.

With only three weeks or so left in the season, everyone fighting to get home would take every single battle seriously.

"So what's the plan, Grey?" Kiri said. He was glad for it, since her words implied he was in charge without him having to say it.

"I don't want us playing overly aggressive today," he started. "Today we need to play smart to hold our ranks. Instead of landing in places with big fights, we need to pick areas where we can loot up well so we can be stocked for end-of-battle fights. I'm thinking Shifty Shafts for the first game. We have a lot of rotation options after that."

Finn nodded. "That's a decent place, yeah, but if another squad shows up, we could be in trouble."

"That's always a risk anywhere," Kiri said.

"Yeah, but we can keep an eye on landings," Grey said. "Shifty Shafts, Fatal Fields, maybe Risky Reels or Lucky Landing, if the Battle Bus takes a decent path across them. We all need to stock up on mats. Just so you guys know, Kiri always gets priority on best snipers. But other than that, we try to divide the loot by who needs stuff or if someone has room to carry bandages or shields."

"Are you gonna tell us what to build?" Hazel asked. "Like, just how bossy are you?"

"Not always," Grey said. "I often ask if people have picked up launch pads or traps or bounce pads, but not as much on how to build your structures."

"You need to defend yourself," Kiri said. "Sometimes he would tell our old squad mates to flank or break a structure or something like that. But they would often ask to do something, and he'd approve it."

"Yeah," Grey said. "We all just need to be on the same page, okay? I don't want to stop you from playing well—you are both great players—but we have to find the best way for us to work as a team, you know?"

Everyone nodded.

"I'm not gonna lie," he continued. "I don't know the exact best way for us to play together yet. We're all gonna make mistakes today. I won't kick anyone out for mistakes. But we all have to try and listen to each other."

Hazel sighed. "This kumbaya stuff is going to kill me."

"You wanted to join," Kiri said.

Hazel held up her hands. "I know, I know. Let's just kick some butt, okay?"

"Heck, yeah," Finn said. He glanced at Grey. "*While* listening."

"Sounds great to me," Grey said with a smile. Even if everyone thought their squad was a strange combination, he knew they could find a way to make it work.

Soon they were all teleported to their ranking line to start the day. The Admin appeared before them, "Welcome to Day Thirty-Five of Battles! The map remains the same, but we have resolved the bug submitted by Martine concerning the reload time on blue SMG. It was slightly faster than the other SMGs and has now been made the same as the others. We thank Martine for her acute observation skills. Good luck—especially to our new player, Finn—in your battles today."

The first battle will begin in thirty seconds!

Grey took a deep breath as he prepared to be transported to the Battle Bus. Adrenaline coursed through him, and his mind raced over all the ways today could go wrong. But he tried to push those out and find the good.

He had a full squad again.

His best friend was here.

They all were hungry to win.

When they arrived in the Battle Bus, Grey immediately looked at the map to see which direction the bus was headed over the island. It was going south to north on the east side—not a great path for their planned location of Shifty Shafts.

"Change of plans," Grey said. "Let's try Risky Reels and rotate to Tomato Town from there."

"Good idea," Finn said. "Shifty would be dismal at this angle."

Lots of players jumped long before they did, and Grey paid attention to where they were flying. It seemed like half were going Retail Row or Salty Springs, so those two places would be madhouses. But it might work for them—lots of early eliminations meant they'd get a higher rank just by taking their time.

"Going in three . . . two . . . one!" Grey jumped from the bus with the rest of his squad. There were a few people in the air with them, but they ventured off toward Tomato Town or the shipping container yard.

No one followed them to Risky Reels.

It was a boring way to land, but a safe way. The rickety drive-in movie theater had plenty of loot and materials for them, even if it didn't have much action. And they even found a llama on their way out to help stock them up with materials, traps, a campfire, and a handful of bounce pads.

Then there was the storm. They were outside the next circle that bordered Anarchy Acres, and they would need to keep their eyes open while making the trek that direction.

"Almost everyone will be coming in from the south," Grey said as they ran toward the new radius of the safe zone. "Probably those two from Tomato Town first."

"Right," Hazel said. "We got lucky on the storm."

They did. Chances were, they'd be the first ones to the safe zone. If they were careful and observant, they could get the jump on anyone running in. But they would need the materials and the loot to be able to keep fighting.

"Just make sure you're stocked up for building," Grey said. "We'll loot more in Anarchy Acres."

"Two incoming," Finn declared. "Permission to open fire?"

"Yeah, let's get 'em." Grey had spotted the two people even though they tried to duck behind the trees to hide. "Finn, you can go aggressive. We'll back you up."

"Sweet!" Finn happily took the front position.

Grey wanted to see how Finn could play in the open field, since he remembered Finn being good at that. The risk was low, as this duo was outnumbered and likely not high ranked. There were still sixty people in play, since the first storm was just about to close in.

The duo opened fire on them, but Finn used walls to protect himself. Building their own walls and ramps from protection, the duo came at them with surprising aggression. Grey used the basic SMG he'd gotten to put pressure on them, breaking down their walls with speed. Finn used a shotgun for higher damage, and soon both the players fell to the ground.

Finn eliminated Anya.

You eliminated Veejay.

Finn used a dance emote to proclaim his victory. "Wewt! First elimination in virtual reality."

"Don't get too excited," Hazel said. "Those

two are a couple now—they're tanking their scores on purpose."

"Oh . . . way to ruin it," Finn replied.

"Sorry," Grey said. "Told you this version was weird.

As they began to look through Veejay's and Anya's loot, Hazel took damage to her shield. Grey reflexively put up a wall as more shots poured in. "I see three at least! Southwest!"

"No, there's four!" Kiri said as she looked through her sniper scope.

Grey began to build up a tower, since the area where they were was mostly open field and trees. They weren't quite in the safe zone of the storm, and it would start to close soon. This needed to be a fast fight. "Time to push before the storm gets us."

"You think?" Hazel followed him up the ramps. "Should I grenade or save them?"

Grey didn't want to waste the grenade launcher shots so early on, but he also didn't want to get stuck in the storm. Especially when there were still so many squads to face. They had to at least make it to the top thirty this battle and every battle, if not better, if they wanted to have a fighting chance to get home.

"Yeah, use it. Hopefully we'll find more ammo at Anarchy."

Hazel launched several grenades at the squad, laying waste to their walls as Finn and Grey tried to keep up the pressure.

But the team was building fast, and the walls kept coming back up just before Grey's enemies were exposed.

Kiri knocked down Julio.

"It's Lorenzo's squad!" Kiri said as she took another shot through her scope. "We got this, guys!"

Kiri eliminated Julio.

"Are you human?" Finn cried. "You got him in two shots!"

"Kiri is the sniper queen," Grey said. "C'mon, let's push hard. They have to be hurting from those 'nades—we can't give them time to heal up."

"I got those bouncers," Finn offered.

"Save them," Grey replied. "We might need it later."

Finn sighed. But he didn't use it. Grey didn't like knowing Finn disagreed with him, but he'd have to get used to it because they had different styles. "Can I at least use my impulse 'nades?"

"Sure," Grey conceded. Impulse grenades didn't do damage, but they did make a player fly. But unlike a bounce pad, that player could also take fall damage if they fell from too high. They were risky in a big build battle, but right now Grey's squad wasn't too far off the ground.

"Me too!" Hazel insisted.

"Pull the flank then!" Grey called. Maybe if he let those two be aggressive now, they'd get it out of their systems and be focused later on against harder squads. Tae Min's advice of "don't be soft" crossed Grey's mind . . . He wasn't doing that.

"Going!" Finn moved close to Hazel and used his impulse grenade to launch them into the air. They flew over Lorenzo's buildings, all the while shooting as they went.

Since all of Lorenzo's squad hid behind the walls, Grey focused on bringing them down with Kiri, hoping to see elimination announcements from his more aggressive squad mates. The gunfire was loud and constant, and he could see their avatars jumping as they attempted to avoid damage.

Hazel knocked down Coco.

Selena knocked down Hazel.

Grey began to panic. He couldn't lose Hazel so early on. "Focus on the damagers, Finn! We're coming!"

"I'll protect you, Hazel!" Finn cried.

Grey hoped he would. Getting downed this early would eat up a lot of their supplies as they made sure Hazel was healthy for the next fight. *If* she had a next fight. The risk of elimination was still high.

Grey was almost out of ammo on his SMG, so he switched to the AR he had even though the damage wasn't as good. The walls broke down, exposing Selena and Julio from behind. Grey switched weapons again to his hunting rifle and opened fire on the avatar dressed like a pink teddy bear.

You knocked down Selena.

Kiri eliminated Lorenzo by head shot.

Finn eliminated Coco.

With Coco eliminated, Selena was also automatically eliminated since there was no one standing to revive her.

"Reviving Hazel!" Finn was already by Hazel's green-haired avatar.

Grey quickly threw up some walls to protect them while she was revived. "Hurry and grab everything we can carry. We used a lot of resources."

"More than we should have, probably." Hazel's voice sounded upset but not angry. For a second, Grey thought she might have sounded insecure. "Thanks for the revive . . . My old squad had a left-for-dead policy."

"Really?" Kiri said as she grabbed more sniper ammo and refilled her shield with what their opponents had dropped.

"Yeah," Hazel said. "They weren't about to help your rank if you couldn't stay alive."

"Wait, your whole squad doesn't get the same rank?" Finn asked.

"Nah, not like the usual game." Hazel bandaged herself once she was revived. "The moment you're eliminated, that's your rank no matter how far your squad gets."

"Dang," Finn said. "This place is so cutthroat."

Grey hadn't realized that was different, since he'd never played before getting stuck here. It would have been nice if squads could carry your rank, but he could see why that wouldn't work in this version.

The storm moves in one minute and thirty seconds.

"We need to get going." Grey picked up the remaining small shield potions and the extra small ammo for his SMG. There was plenty of building materials left from the eliminated players, and he took them all for time's sake. They could redistribute later if needed.

As the storm shrunk the map, the number of remaining players shrunk as well. He could imagine the fights going on as people raced to get into the next safe zone.

Just about forty players remained as they made it to Anarchy Acres. Ben and Tristan hadn't been eliminated yet. Today was the first day Grey felt like he could face them again, and he had a feeling the battle would be fierce. All he could hope was that they'd survive it.

CHAPTER 12

Anarchy Acres was quiet when they arrived, but Grey knew that wouldn't last forever. Loot Lake and Dusty Divot were still within the safe zone, so some players may have stopped there to loot up or fight, but the next storm radius would cut out most of those areas as well. Anarchy Acres would still be in the safe circle, as well as the northwestern parts of the island.

The farm was completely untouched, which was good for Grey's squad because they needed all the resources they could get for the upcoming fights. While it wasn't the most entertaining to farm materials and loot chests, Grey had his team spread out over Anarchy Acres to do just that.

"Everyone needs max wood at least," he said

as he broke down fences. "Max brick wouldn't hurt, either."

"Not much metal here," Finn said. "But there is at Junk Junction if we plan to move there."

"Right." Grey hadn't decided where to go after Anarchy Acres. It depended on how the storm shrunk the map. If it moved toward Junk Junction, it would be great to get there before anyone else. "Let's see which way the next storm circle moves first, keep an eye on the south for incoming players."

"Alrighty," Finn said. "At max wood. Can I scout?"

"Sure," Grey said.

"I'll go with him," Hazel said. "I'm at max, too."

"Okay." Grey still wasn't confident in splitting up the squad, but he figured that was something he needed to practice. And it did seem like Finn and Hazel made a pretty strong pair. They had taken too much damage in the last fight, but they had ultimately won it. He had to try and trust in their different styles of playing.

"See anything?" Kiri asked as she continued to break down some rocks for brick.

"Big builds at Loot Lake," Finn said. "Think the fight is still going."

"One incoming from Dusty Divot!" Hazel announced. "Permission to fight?"

Grey hesitated, since he couldn't see what they did. But then he said, "As long as it's you and Finn. There could be more."

"C'mon, Finn!" Hazel ran toward Dusty Divot, with Finn right behind her. He appreciated that she was at least making an effort to ask and be part of the squad. He wasn't sure, after all of Hazel's trolling, that she was capable of working so well with other people.

Grey couldn't see what was happening, but he did hear shots echo through the area as Hazel's health bar dropped.

"What the . . . ?" Fin cried as the notification read: *Tae Min eliminated Hazel.*

"No!" Kiri yelled. "Run, Finn!"

"I got this!" Finn said.

"Get out!" Grey yelled. "He's the best player in the—"

Tae Min eliminated Finn by head shot.

Grey and Kiri were already running. All they could hope at this point was that Tae Min would run into another group before he got to them. There was a decent amount of distance, but it was Finn who had carried their bounce pads.

Now Tae Min had the bounce pads and, if he spotted them, could easily use them to catch up to Grey and Kiri.

"Sorry, guys," Grey said as he looked behind him. "I expected Tae Min to be around Loot Lake—he favors Tilted Towers."

"He totally does," Hazel said. "And he was wearing a default skin to trick us!"

"I still don't understand how I was eliminated . . ." Finn said quietly. "I didn't hit him once."

"He's Tae Min," Kiri said.

"He's the god of this world," Hazel said. "I'll spectate him and report. He's moving toward the builds at Loot Lake."

Grey felt a wave a relief. Maybe they were down two squad members, but if Hazel was willing to keep an eye on Tae Min, it would help Grey and Kiri get a few more ranks before they met their demise. "Thanks for watching out for us. I know you don't have to do that."

"I'd want you to do it if I were the one left alive," Hazel said.

With just under forty players left and the storm closing in again, Grey had to form a plan. While he felt guilty for not expecting that solo player to be Tae Min, he couldn't do anything about it now. He'd felt too much pressure to let Finn and Hazel do their thing—he needed to be better about keeping them all together. It was his mistake, and he wouldn't make it again.

When the storm began to shrink again, it stayed over the Anarchy Acres area. Grey and Kiri took shelter in the broken-down motel west of the farm as they watched the eliminations on the map pile up. It was a cowardly strategy, but Grey was panicked by the early loss of half his squad. He wasn't sure what to do next.

In the time Grey sat around thinking, fifteen people got eliminated either in fights or in the storm. The remaining players would definitely be converging on their position soon.

"How about we build a tower?" Kiri said. "This area is a little flat."

"Right." Grey was glad someone could think straight. He began his build right on top of the motel, and putting down walls and ramps helped him get out of his funk. At least until he saw the next eliminations.

Tae Min eliminated Zach.

Tae Min knocked down Hui Yin.

"That's Ben and Tristan's squad!" Kiri said as she peered out over the ledge of their tower.

Grey held his breath as he waited to see them get downed. Maybe it wasn't him doing the eliminating, but it would still be nice to know he outranked them in this battle. But the notification didn't come.

"They got Tae Min in a crazy build battle!" Hazel said. "They had the gall to try and trap him. He didn't fall for it."

"I'm watching Ben," Finn said. "They have the high ground on him."

Tae Min eliminated Hui Yin.

"These guys are boxing in," Finn reported. "They're low on health."

"They're done for," Hazel said. "Tae Min won't let them heal."

"Ben is waiting to edit the wall . . ." Finn said. "The other guy has an impulse grenade out."

Grey's eyes went wide as he realized what his old squad mates were planning. "Are they seriously . . . How high up are they?"

"Really high," Hazel said. "At least eight stacks."

"They're gonna impulse Tae Min off the tower," Grey said. He knew they would because that's what he would have done in that situation. There was no other way to fight Tae Min fairly—he would out-aim and out-build you every time. The only way to have any hope was some kind of ridiculous trick. The trap didn't work, so this was the next thing he'd do.

"No way!" Hazel squealed. "They sent him flying!"

Tae Min didn't stick the landing.

Grey imagined that everyone watching was impressed with Ben and Tristan, but it only made him angry. They wouldn't have thought of that tactic without the time they'd spent with Grey. They were using his ideas. They were ranking up because of what he'd taught them, and now they were taking out the top player without Grey.

He wouldn't let Ben and Tristan get away with it.

"Where are they now?" Grey asked.

"Moving your way," Finn said. "Like just south of the motel."

"Kiri, stay up here. I'm gonna bait them." Grey was already building ramps down from their perch on the tower.

"Grey!" Kiri called. "Don't be stupid! Get back here!"

"They *stole* my ideas." Grey was already on the ground, his mind far past the frozen moments of just before. His ideas could eliminate Tae Min. He never realized that, and he wasn't about to let Ben and Tristan get credit for what he'd taught them.

Grey spotted them on the horizon, and he used his AR to fire on them because that ammo wouldn't be missed. He didn't intend to eliminate them like this—he wanted their attention.

It worked.

They shot back, and he knew they'd use the bounce pads they got off Tae Min. He'd taught them all about offensive bounce pad use. Sure enough, as Grey pretended to box himself in out of fear, they built a ramp and placed a bounce pad down on it.

Grey dropped a trap on the floor of his box and then wasted a lot of shots to make noise in order to hide the sound of the trap forming.

He had to hand it to them—all that practicing they did on bounce pads paid off in their perfect aim landing in the box.

They jumped frantically as they saw the trap, but Grey dropped traps on the walls as well. He shot at them for good measure, but it didn't matter when all the spikes came at his old squad mates.

Grey eliminated Ben.

Grey eliminated Tristan.

Grey used his bowing emote to drive home the point. He hoped everyone was watching, because the revenge felt good.

"*Dannng*, Grey," Hazel said. "Way to make a statement."

"Thanks for keeping an eye out for me," he replied. "I hadn't watched them since they left. I had no idea just how much they were copying my ideas. But I have more ideas, and they can't steal them now."

"That was genius, dude," Finn said. "You read their minds."

Grey and Kiri didn't win the battle, but they made it to the top fifteen. Once the battle was over, people crowded around Grey and his squad to compliment the brilliant outplay. Grey caught Ben and Tristan looking on in embarrassment, and he promised himself he'd never lose his confidence again.

He could lead this new squad to victory. Because it wasn't just his old team's synergy that got them to success—it was his ideas. And he still had plenty of those to spare.